SUPER DC HEROES.

THE

DARK KNIGHT
™

THE JOKER VIRUS

WRITTEN BY
SCOTT PETERSON

ILLUSTRATED BY
MIKE CAVALLARO

BATMAN CREATED BY BOB KANE

STONE ARCH BOOKS

PUBLISHED BY STONE ARCH BOOKS IN 2012
A CAPSTONE IMPRINT
1710 ROE CREST DRIVE
NORTH MANKATO, MN 56003
WWW.CAPSTONEPUB.COM

CATALOGING-IN-PUBLICATION DATA IS AVAILABLE AT THE
LIBRARY OF CONGRESS WEBSITE.

ISBN: 978-1-4342-4096-5 (LIBRARY BINDING)
ISBN: 978-1-4342-4218-1 (PAPERBACK)

SUMMARY: JOKER VENOM HAS GONE VIRAL! WHEN
THE CLOWN PRINCE OF CRIME CREATES A DIGITAL
VERSION OF HIS MOST DANGEROUS WEAPON, MILLIONS
OF VIDEO-GAME PLAYERS BECOME HIS OBEDIENT
ZOMBIES. IF THE DARK KNIGHT CAN'T STOP THIS VIRUS
FROM SPREADING SOON, IT'LL BE GAME OVER FOR
THE WORLD'S GREATEST DETECTIVE.

ART DIRECTOR: BOB LENTZ
DESIGNER: BRANN GARVEY

PRINTED IN THE UNITED STATES OF AMERICA
IN STEVENS POINT, WISCONSIN.

TABLE OF CONTENTS

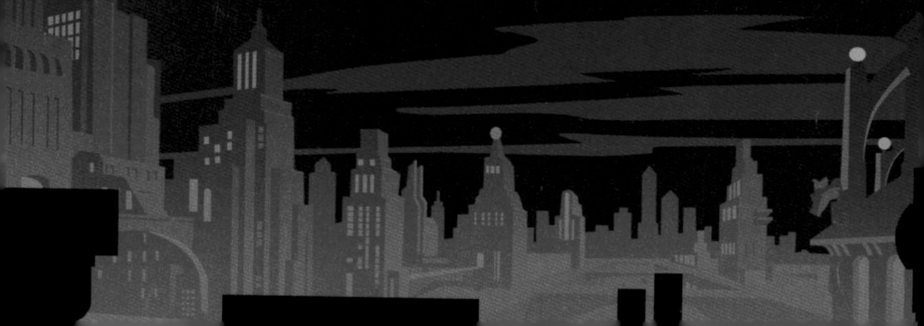

WHILE STILL A BOY, BRUCE WAYNE WITNESSED THE BRUTAL MURDER OF HIS PARENTS. THE TRAGIC EVENT CHANGED THE YOUNG BILLIONAIRE FOREVER. BRUCE VOWED TO RID GOTHAM CITY OF EVIL AND KEEP ITS PEOPLE SAFE FROM CRIME. AFTER YEARS OF TRAINING HIS BODY AND MIND, HE DONNED A NEW UNIFORM AND A NEW IDENTITY.

HE BECAME...

THE

DARK KNIGHT

™

CHAPTER 1

GOTHAM GAMES

"Batman, look out!" Robin's voice called from above.

Batman tensed and listened. He heard a whisper of fabric moving. He felt the tiniest gust of air. Without taking his eyes off the two muggers in front of him, he reached up and behind him. He made contact with the wrist of the third mugger. The one he hadn't seen. The one Robin's yell had warned him about.

Batman tightened his grip around the mugger's wrist.

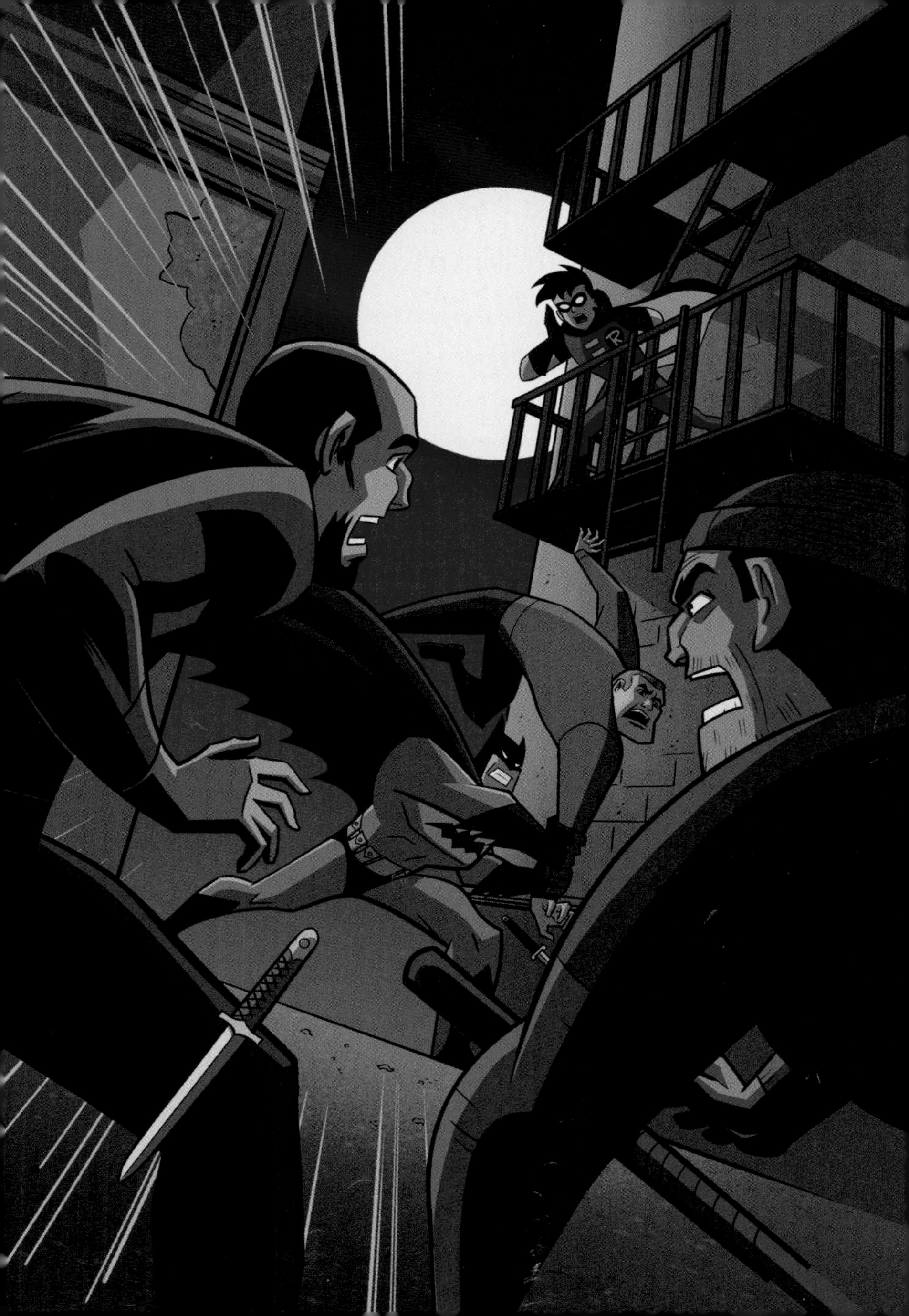

Batman twisted the thief's arm, and the knife dropped out of the mugger's hand. Batman threw the crook over his shoulder, and he hit the alley pavement with a *THUDOOOOO!*

One mugger was down for the count, and the Dark Knight still hadn't even needed to take his eyes off the first two muggers.

"I did that without looking," Batman said to the criminals. "Imagine what I can do with my eyes on you two."

The two muggers shot each other glances. Immediately, they dropped their weapons. Without a word, they placed their hands on their heads, sank to their knees, and stared down at the ground. They'd been arrested before. They knew the drill.

"Don't move," Batman said. The muggers nodded. A few moments later, they looked up to see only darkness. There was no sign the Dark Knight had ever been there.

A moment later, Robin, the Boy Wonder, lightly touched the shoulder of the old lady the muggers had been trying to rob. "Are you okay, ma'am?" he said. "The police are on their way. Is there anyone you'd like me to call for you?"

The woman shook her head. "Thank you, young man, but I'll be fine. Thanks to —" She looked around, intending to thank Batman, but he was nowhere to be seen. "He doesn't waste much time, does he?"

Robin shrugged. "He's a pretty busy guy," he said.

The friendly old lady smiled back. "Well, I appreciate you taking the time to check on me," she said.

Robin smiled. "No problem, ma'am," he said. "Just doing my job."

A pair of police cars screeched to a halt at the entrance to the alley. "Looks like you're all set," Robin said, pointing the lady toward the cops. "Have a nice night."

A moment later, the police arrived at the scene of the attempted crime. There was no sign that Batman or Robin had been there. Except, of course, for the three would-be muggers lying very still — and very frightened — on the cold concrete.

"Is he gone?" one mugger asked nervously.

The lead officer chuckled and slapped a pair of cuffs on the crook. **CLICK! CLICK!**

"Just another Tuesday night in Gotham," the other officer said with a smile.

*   *   *

"Ah, Gotham," the Joker said, laughing. "You never cease to amuse me."

The Clown Prince of Crime glanced around the art museum. Everywhere he looked, he saw paintings of Pagliacci, the famous clown. Surrounding him were countless people — all of them staring at the floor.

"Well, that's not right," the Joker said. "All their eyes should be on me."

He walked over to a short, muscular man dressed in a tuxedo.

"You, there," the Joker said. Slowly, the man looked up. "Yes, you. Why is everyone staring at the floor? Is this some new, modern way of appreciating art?"

"No," the man mumbled. "We're trying to avoid making eye contact with you."

"Ah," the Joker said. "And why might that be?"

"Because we're terrified of you," the man said quietly.

"I see," the Joker said. "Well, that's certainly not unreasonable. In fact, it's quite logical. If you weren't terrified of me, well, you'd simply have to be crazy!" The Joker burst into a maniacal laugh. A sadistic grin crawled across his face. "And I'm afraid I've got the market on 'crazy' cornered."

CLAP! CLAP!

The Joker clapped his hands suddenly. "But I'm afraid this simply won't do," he said. "I like an audience. Everyone look at me. Look at me!"

The Clown Prince of Crime went up on his toes and spun around like an agile ballerina. His shrill voice rang out. "To see the Joker up close and personal like this?" he called out. "It's a once in a lifetime chance — if you're lucky!"

He peered around the room. Every person in the museum now had their eyes trained on him. Not a single pair of eyes blinked. It was obvious he had their full attention.

"Excellent," he cackled. "That's more like it. Now then, I —"

BEEP! BEEP! BEEP!

The Joker froze. He tilted his head, trying to figure out where the sounds had come from.

BEEP! BEEP! BEEP!

The Clown Prince whirled around. He slowly moved across the gallery's enormous floor. On the tips of his toes, he went first this way, and then that way.

BEEP! BEEP! BEEP!

Suddenly he squatted down. Behind a row of legs, he saw a girl and a boy sitting on the floor away from the group. They were playing with a pair of handheld video games.

"And what do we have here?" the Joker purred.

Neither child looked up. "Games," the girl answered.

The Joker smiled. "I love games!" he cried out with childlike glee. "What kind of game are you playing?"

"A video game," the boy said in an annoyed tone.

"Well, obviously," the Joker cooed. "Does this oh-so-captivating video game have a name?"

The girl sighed. "*Ninja Nemesis*," she said. Her voice made it very clear that she thought the question was foolish.

The Joker tapped his chin. "And is this *Ninja Nemesis* game . . . fun?"

Neither child answered. The Joker cleared his throat. Finally, the boy grunted out a, "Yeah."

"More fun," the Joker said, standing up and throwing his arms out triumphantly, "than the Joker?"

The Joker paused, waiting for a response. But when he looked down, he discovered neither child had bothered to look up from their games.

TAP! TAP! TAP! On the boy's screen, a ninja performed a backflip over a speeding vehicle.

The Joker squatted down next to the kids. "Are you telling me that those games are more interesting than the Joker?" he asked.

After another pause, the girl asked, "Who's the Joker?"

"Who's the . . . who's the Joker?!" the super-villain sputtered.

"Oh, my poor, dear neglected child," Joker said. "What do they teach you in schools these days? Have your parents taught you nothing? Reading, writing, criminal masterminds who prey on the innocent?"

The girl shrugged. Still not looking up, the boy said, "We don't really pay much attention to politics."

The Joker went still. Then he stood. He slowly counted to ten. Then, taking a very deep breath, he shrieked.

AHHHHHHHHHHHHHHHH!

The eyes of each adult in the room grew very wide. Every person held their breath. The silence was deafening. The Joker's eyes twitched in anticipation of a fearful response from the kids.

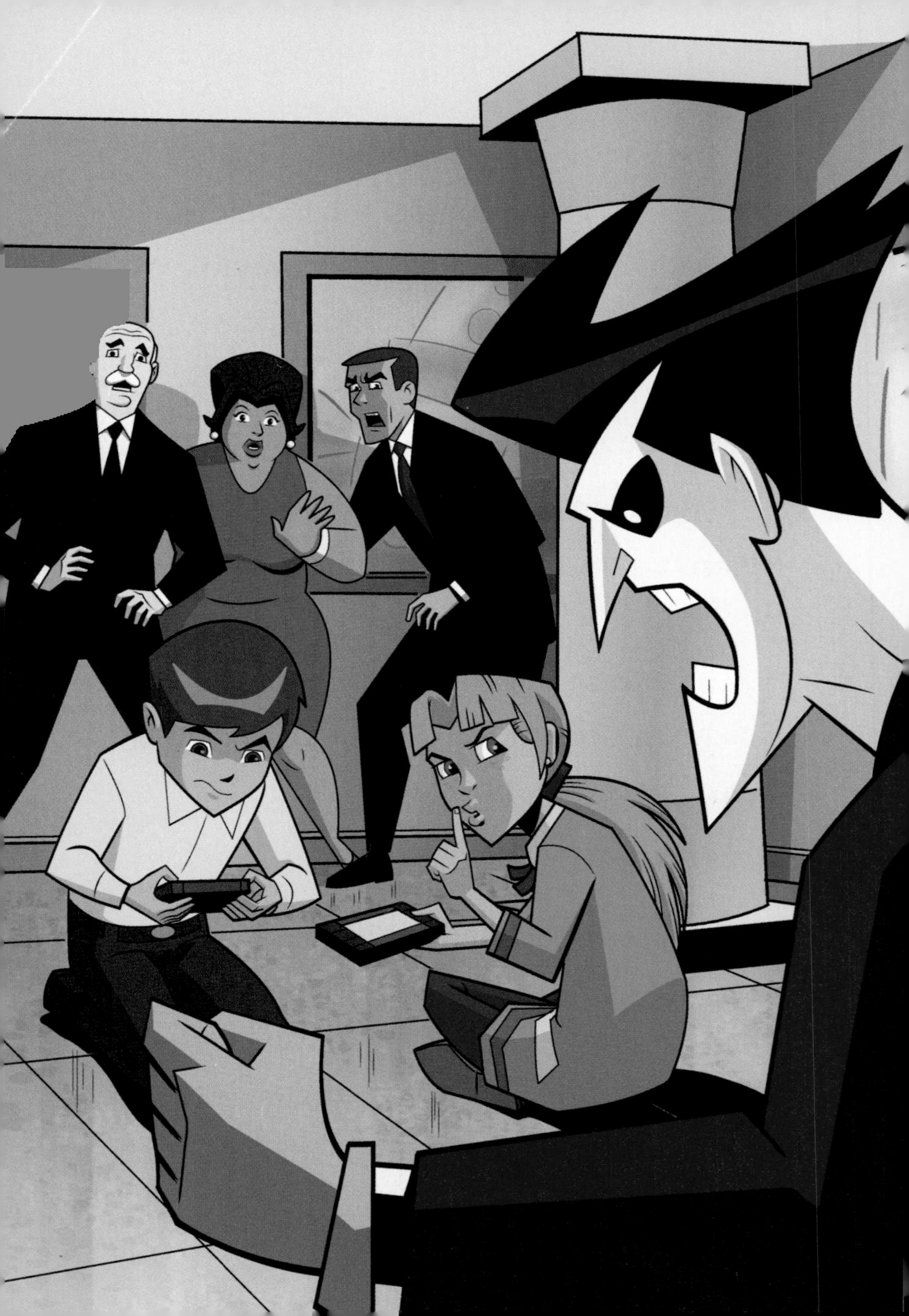

Then the little girl spoke. "Shhh," she said to the Joker. "This is a really tricky level of the game."

The Clown Prince of Crime began to shake with rage. "I'll show you a tricky level!" he screamed.

The boy furrowed his brow. "That doesn't even make sense," he said.

The Joker opened his mouth to reply, but slowly shut it again when he couldn't think of anything witty to say. He turned on his heel and walked very quickly toward the door.

"Well, this didn't go as I'd hoped," Joker grumbled. "An entire lovely evening of total mayhem ruined — simply ruined — by a pair of little brats. Monsters like that are the reason I never had my own children."

The Joker stopped and turned around. He glared at all the frightened faces watching him. "Don't look at me!" he roared.

Every eye instantly stared down at the floor. No one said a word.

"Hmph," the Joker said. "At least the adults are still scared of me."

He stopped and scratched his chin. He paced back and forth. "What am I supposed to do next?" he wondered aloud. "I feel like I've lost my focus. Maybe I should just go home."

SLAM!

Joker pushed open the doors and marched out of the museum. But a few feet outside, the Joker stopped again. He snapped his fingers.

"I forgot to dose them all with my Joker Venom," he said in a sour voice. "Sigh. A joker's job is never done."

Joker turned around to face the museum. He ran his hands through his hair. "What is happening to me?" he wondered. "One little pair of video game playing brats has totally thrown me off my, um . . . game."

The super-villain grew very still. Slowly, a terrible smile crawled across his bright red lips.

"Oh," he said softly. "If kids love their precious little video games so much, then I'll give them the greatest game of all!"

HAHAHAHHAHAHAHA!

The Joker's cackling laughter filtered back into the museum. Every person inside who heard it would have nightmares for weeks.

And that's exactly what the Joker wanted.

CHAPTER 2

DIGITAL DANGER

RUMBBBBBBBLE!

The Batmobile roared into the Batcave. Batman killed the engine, and then he started the computer's diagnostic sequence.

By the time the Dark Knight had leaped out of the car, Robin had already changed out of his uniform, jumped into his civilian clothes, and walked halfway up the steps leading to Wayne Manor.

Alfred Pennyworth, their trusty butler and confidant, was just coming down the stairs. "Good morning, Master Timothy," he said.

"Good morning, Alfred," Robin said excitedly. "Did you remember to take care of —?"

"Yes," Alfred said before the Boy Wonder could finish.

"And did you get the package I —?" Robin began.

"Of course," Alfred interrupted again.

"Yes!" Robin agreed. He sprinted up the stairs past a smiling Alfred.

Batman watched him go with a grin. Then the hero began his regular early morning routine.

Every dawn, after returning from another night of being Batman, the Dark Knight scanned each major newspaper in the world and used his secret log in and password to check Gotham City's police reports for the previous twelve hours.

"What was that all about?" Batman asked Alfred.

"Young Timothy was wondering if Gotham Express had arrived yet with a package he's been eagerly awaiting," the butler explained. "It has."

"Kind of early for deliveries, isn't it?" Batman asked.

"Indeed it is, Master Bruce," the butler agreed. "But apparently this is the latest ultra-popular video game. The most anticipated game of the year, if I recall correctly."

"So much so that mail services have had to add extra drivers and expand their normal delivery hours," Alfred said. "The games went on sale precisely at midnight last night."

Batman shook his head. "I don't get the appeal," he said. "Then again, I never was much for games, was I, Alfred?"

The butler smiled sadly. "Not really, sir, no," he said. "Even before you became Batman, you always did tend to be a rather . . . serious boy."

Batman nodded. "Well, if it makes Tim happy, then I guess that's what matters," he said. "He has enough on his plate just being Robin. It's probably a good thing he gets some time to just be a teenager again."

Alfred began to dust the enormous Batcomputer. "Quite so," he said. He glanced up at the Batcomputer to see a variety of files open on the Joker. "No sign yet of the Clown Prince, I take it?"

"No," the Batman said in a grim voice. "It's been more than three weeks since his . . . attack, or whatever it was, at the museum's grand opening. It's not like him to go silent this long. I don't like it."

Alfred sensed his friend was upset. "You miss your nemesis, sir?" he joked, trying to lighten the mood.

"Very funny, Alfred," Batman replied. "He could be anywhere, doing anything right now. But he doesn't normally take this long to hatch a plan. It makes me very nervous."

"No chance he's decided to simply quit, I suppose," Alfred said, dusting away.

"No," Batman said. "I think it's just the opposite. The long delay makes me think he's got something big planned."

Alfred nodded. "A distinct possibility," he said.

Batman finished reading the major news stories from around the world and turned his attention to last night's police reports. He flipped back to a previous one and studied it more closely. Then he began moving through the more recent police reports, faster and faster.

"Well," Batman said quietly. "It seems the wait may be over."

"The Joker, sir?" Alfred asked, now reading the screen himself.

"It looks that way," the Batman said. "The police don't seem to have connected the dots quite yet. Or maybe they don't want to start a panic before they know what's going on."

"What *is* going on, sir?" Alfred asked.

"Joker Venom," Batman said grimly. "Reports are popping up everywhere."

Batman slowly clenched his fist. "Look at this," he said.

Batman pulled up a photo on the Batcomputer's screen of a college student. The young man had the telltale look of a Joker victim: his lips were pulled back in a hideous grin, he was paralyzed, and he laughed maniacally. "There have already been dozens of cases reported just like this in Bristol, Devil's Square, Gotham Heights, Newtown, the Bowery . . ."

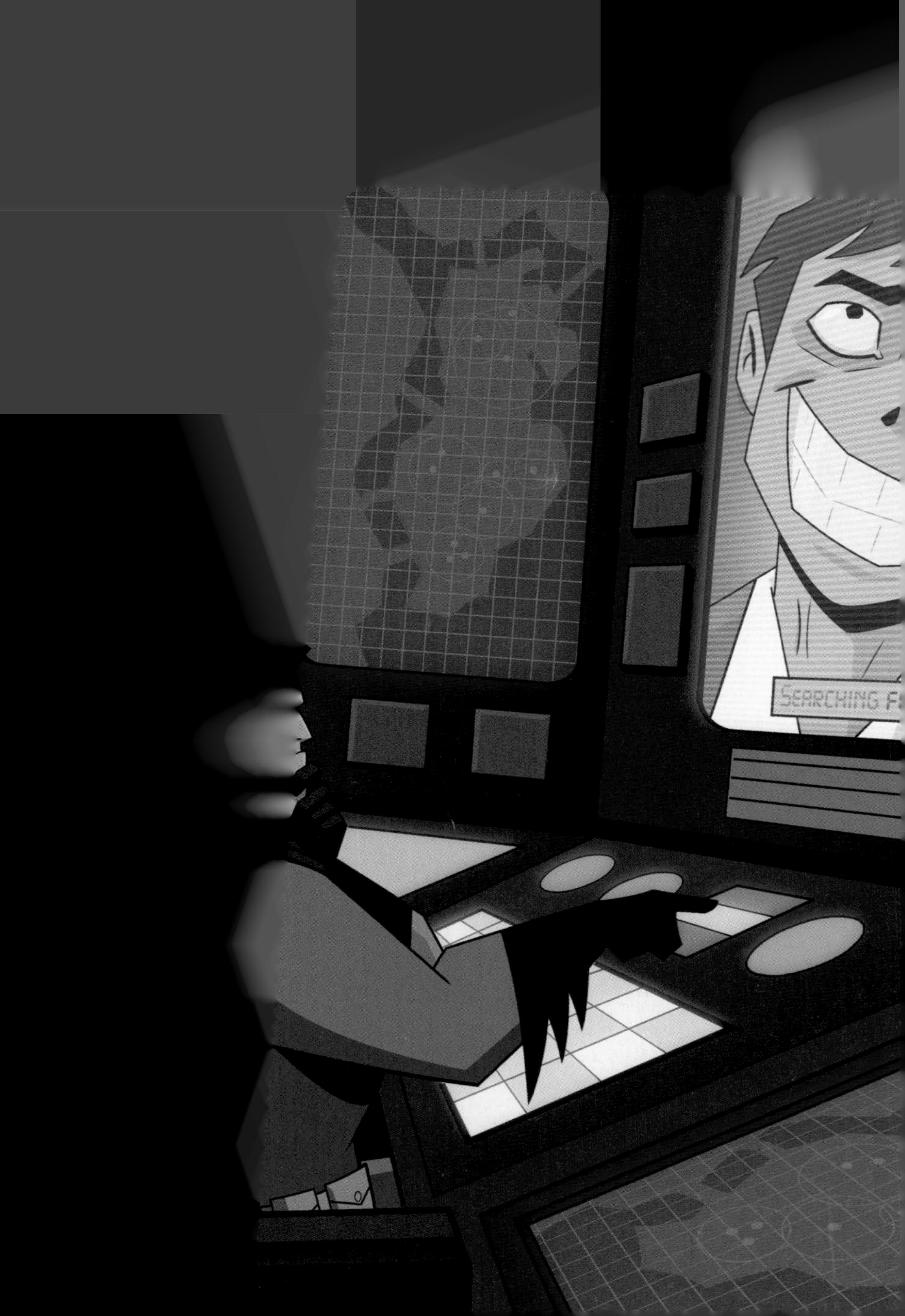
SEARCHING F

Batman began to pace back and forth. "It's happening all over Gotham," Batman said. "In the nicest neighborhoods and the worst areas — and everywhere in between."

"And how are they being dosed with the Joker Venom, sir?" Alfred asked.

"That's just it, Alfred," Batman said. "There hasn't been one report of the Joker — not a single sighting."

"So, the victims are still . . .?" Alfred began.

"At home, yes," Batman finished. "Or in restaurants. Stores. On the bus or the subway. How is that even possible?"

Batman walked over to several targets set up around the Batcave. He picked up a few spare Batarangs and began throwing them at one of the targets.

CLANK! CLINK! CLANK!

As the sharp metal boomerangs hit bull's-eye after bull's-eye, Batman concentrated on identifying patterns. He thought out possible explanations. "What does the Joker have in store for Gotham City this time?" he wondered aloud.

CLANKKKKKKKKK! Suddenly, he stopped throwing Batarangs. He dashed over to the Batcomputer and pulled up the reports again. "Stores!" he said. "That's it!"

"A breakthrough, Master Bruce?" Alfred asked.

Batman nodded, and a hint of a smile crossed his face. "Several of the cases were reported in different stores," he said. "But all the stores sell the same kind of product." He turned toward Alfred. "All the stores sell video games."

"I see!" Alfred said. "So the Joker must have found some way to infect video game players with his Joker Venom."

The Batman fell silent. His eyes went wide. Then, to Alfred's amazement, he did something he never did. He ran upstairs to Wayne Manor while still wearing his Batman uniform.

"Oh, no," Alfred whispered in horror. "Master Timothy!" Dropping his feather duster, the butler sprinted for the stairs.

When Alfred entered Wayne Manor, all was silent. There was no sign of Master Bruce or Master Timothy.

With a feeling of horror growing in his heart, Alfred made his way up toward Master Timothy's room. There he found what he had hoped he would not.

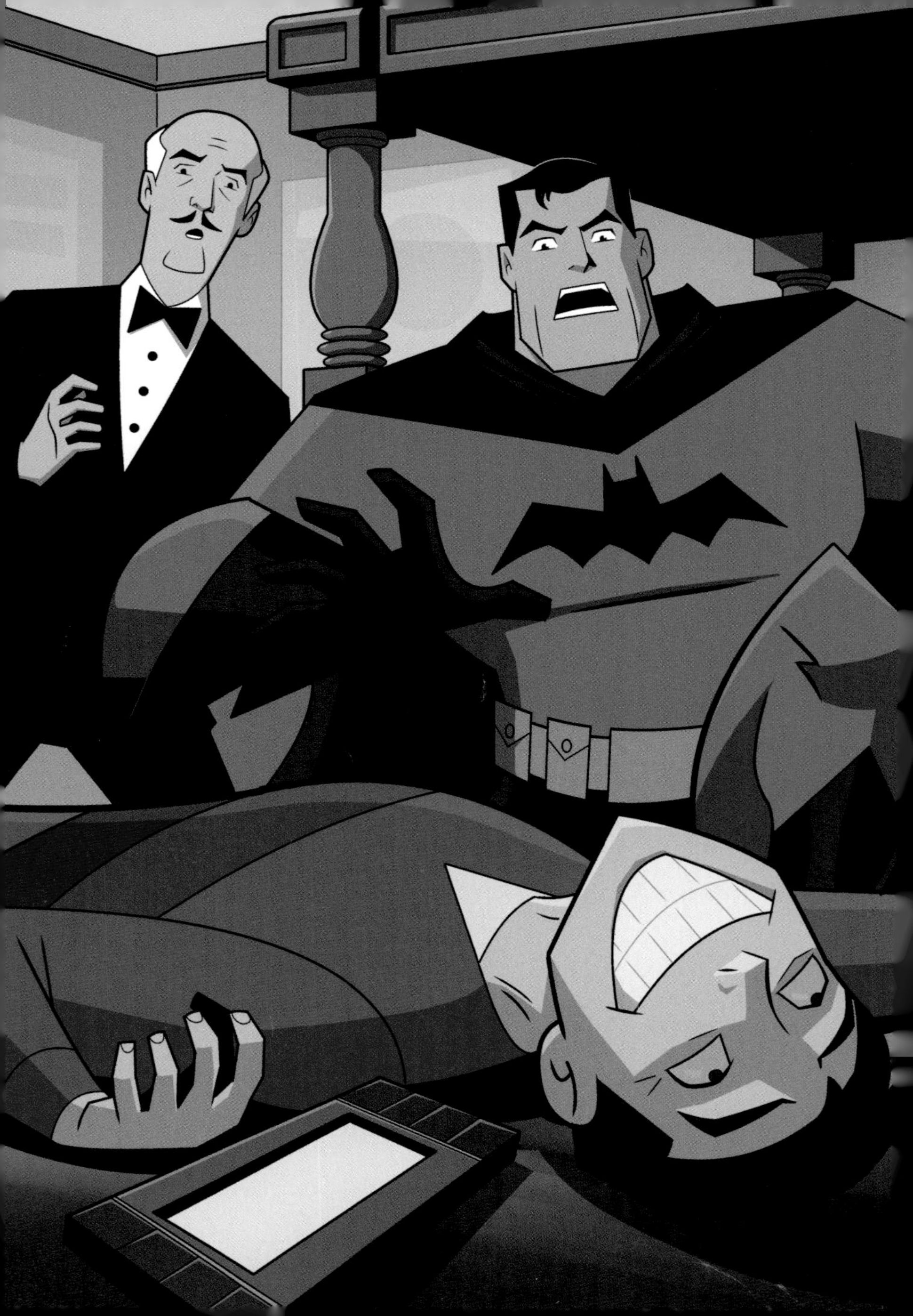

Batman was kneeling next to Master Timothy's motionless body. He was lying on the floor. A Joker grin was spread across his face.

CHAPTER 3

DEAD END

"Jim," a gravelly voice spoke through the receiver.

"Batman," Police Commissioner James Gordon said. Even over the phone, the Dark Knight could tell Gordon was surprised. "I don't normally hear from you while the sun is still up."

"This couldn't wait," Bruce Wayne said in Batman's voice. He looked out the limousine window, watching as the hospital disappeared in the distance.

Bruce and Alfred had rushed Tim to the emergency room. The doctors had run every test they could think of, but Tim's condition didn't get any better. He remained frozen, apparently unconscious, with that terrible grin on his face.

"I take it you've figured out that the Joker is behind all these reports," Commissioner Gordon said. "Any idea how he's doing it, or what the link is between all the victims? They're everywhere, and they don't seem to have anything in common: young and old, rich and poor . . . What ties all these threads together?"

"Games," Bruce said grimly.

"Well, of course," Commissioner Gordon said impatiently. "It's always a game to the Joker. But I meant —"

"No," Bruce interrupted him. "The Joker's using video games to spread his venom."

There was silence for a moment. "That's brilliant," the commissioner admitted. "And pretty sick — even for the Joker."

"Do you have any leads?" Bruce asked.

"Other than the one you just gave us?" Commissioner Gordon said. "No, nothing."

"Well, here's one more," added Bruce. "It might be a game called . . ." He covered the phone with his hand and tapped Alfred on the shoulder.

The butler turned back from the driver's seat and whispered, "*Ninja Nemesis*, sir."

"Are you still there, Batman?" Gordon's muffled voice asked.

"*Ninja Nemesis*," Bruce said. "The game is called *Ninja Nemesis.*"

"Great," Commissioner Gordon said. "Half my officers' kids have already bought that game. Why, even my daughter Barbara was trying to get me to — oh, no! I have to go!"

CLICK! The call ended.

Bruce pulled up the limo's computer and quickly began searching online. "*Ninja Nemesis*," he read. "Gaming sensation . . . has sold more than thirty million copies. Great." He took a deep breath. "Available on dozens of platforms, from desktop computers to phones. A hit on every continent."

Bruce looked over at his oldest friend. "This may be the Joker's most sinister plan ever, and I don't know anything about video games," he admitted. "Robin's the expert gamer, not me. If only he hadn't . . ." Bruce trailed off.

"I know it's difficult," Alfred said. "But you can do this, sir — you always have before."

As the butler turned into Wayne Manor's enormous driveway, he added, "And Master Timothy needs you to do so once more."

Bruce nodded. He turned back to the computer. "Designed by someone named . . . Jonathan Young."

Bruce jumped out of the limo. He ran down to the Batcave. A moment later, Batman leaped into the Batmobile.

VROOOOOOM!

He gunned the engine and peeled out. As the Batmobile made its way out of the cave and into the night, Batman said, "Time to pay Mr. Young a visit."

*   *   *

Batman's research told him that Jonathan Young was one of the videogaming world's biggest stars. As a game designer, one of the most closely guarded secrets in the world was what his next game would be. Even Young's whereabouts at any given time were known to only a handful of people.

The Dark Knight was now one of those people. There was very little that could be kept secret from the World's Greatest Detective.

From a shadow across the street, Batman looked up at Jonathan Young's brownstone building. It was a simple two-story apartment building in a nice, but not fancy, section of the Gotham. In fact, it looked like thousands of other buildings in the city.

With his uncanny speed, Batman glided across the street, blending into the alley beside the building as he soared. He made his way around back. He passed a pair of cats but was so silent that they didn't even look up.

Batman investigated the brownstone from the rear entrance. The building was dark inside and nothing seemed out of place. There were no broken windows or damaged locks.

He began to reach for the back door handle — then stopped. Something felt wrong. Batman had learned years ago to trust his instincts. Slowly, he touched the knob with one finger. *ZAPPPPPPPPPPPP!*

Batman jerked his hand back as a small shock went through his body. The hero smiled. The door was electrified. *Good thing I didn't grab it,* he thought.

The extra security meant Batman's hunch was correct. This had to be the place.

Batman found the building's electrical source.

SNAPPPPPP! He cut it, and then quickly climbed up the side of the building. Once on the roof, the Dark Knight found a skylight. Inside, all was dark and silent.

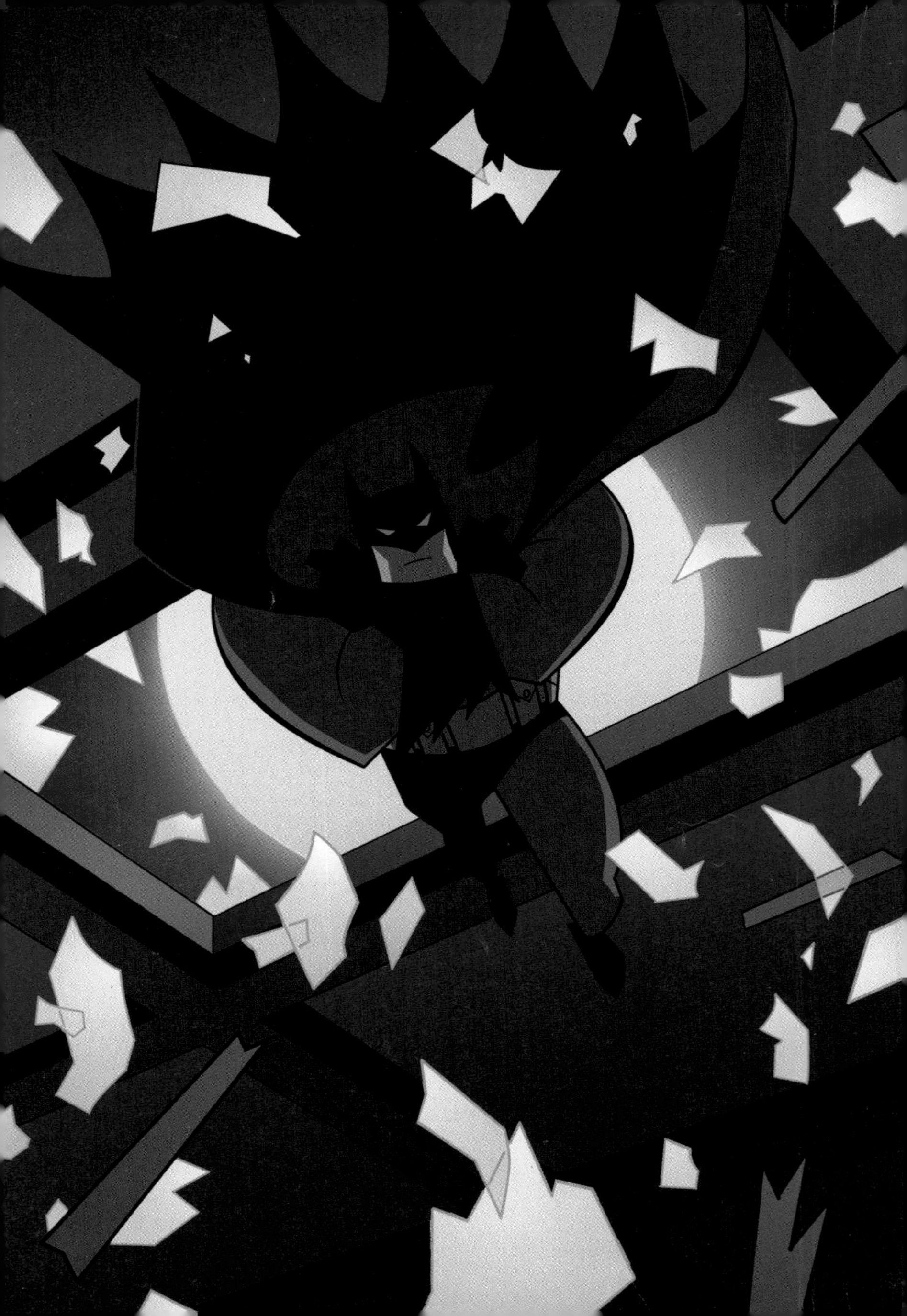

Batman turned on his night vision and jumped in.

CRASSSSSSSSSSSSSSSSSSH! The skylight shattered as the Dark Knight's boots smashed through the glass. Glittering shards dropped down with him on his descent into the dark building.

THUDDDDDDDDDDDDDDDD!

Batman hit the floor and immediately went into a roll. In one deft movement, he sprang back up to his feet and into a battle stance with his fists raised. He waited.

Nothing happened. It was completely silent. Silent except for the slightest hum. A hum so quiet that most anyone would have missed it. But not Batman.

The Dark Knight made his way through the top floor of the house.

Nothing seemed out of place. Nothing, except a mug that had been tipped over on a desk. Batman touched the spilled liquid. It was cold. He smelled it. Hot chocolate. He'd read hot cocoa was a favorite of Jonathan Young's. It didn't seem likely that a game designer would leave liquid spilled near a computer.

Mr. Young had left in a hurry.

Batman looked around the rest of the apartment. He noticed a door that led to a closet. *CLICKKKK!* Inside, the closet seemed smaller than it should have been. Batman moved a few boxes and pressed on the obvious false wall. *CLICKKKKKK!*

"Bingo," Batman said as he opened the hidden door.

Soft blue light poured out the door.

Batman saw dozens of television screens. On each screen was a different view of the brownstone building he was in. On one of the screens, Batman could see himself approaching the computers.

He sat down in a chair. Within moments, the Dark Knight had figured out how to run the surveillance cameras backward. He rewound them to the day after the Joker's museum heist.

Before his eyes, Batman watched the Clown Prince of Crime break in and kidnap Jonathan Young.

Here was proof that the Joker had him and that he likely had forced Mr. Young to cooperate with his evil scheme. Yet Batman was no closer to figuring out where they were. Or how he was going to find them.

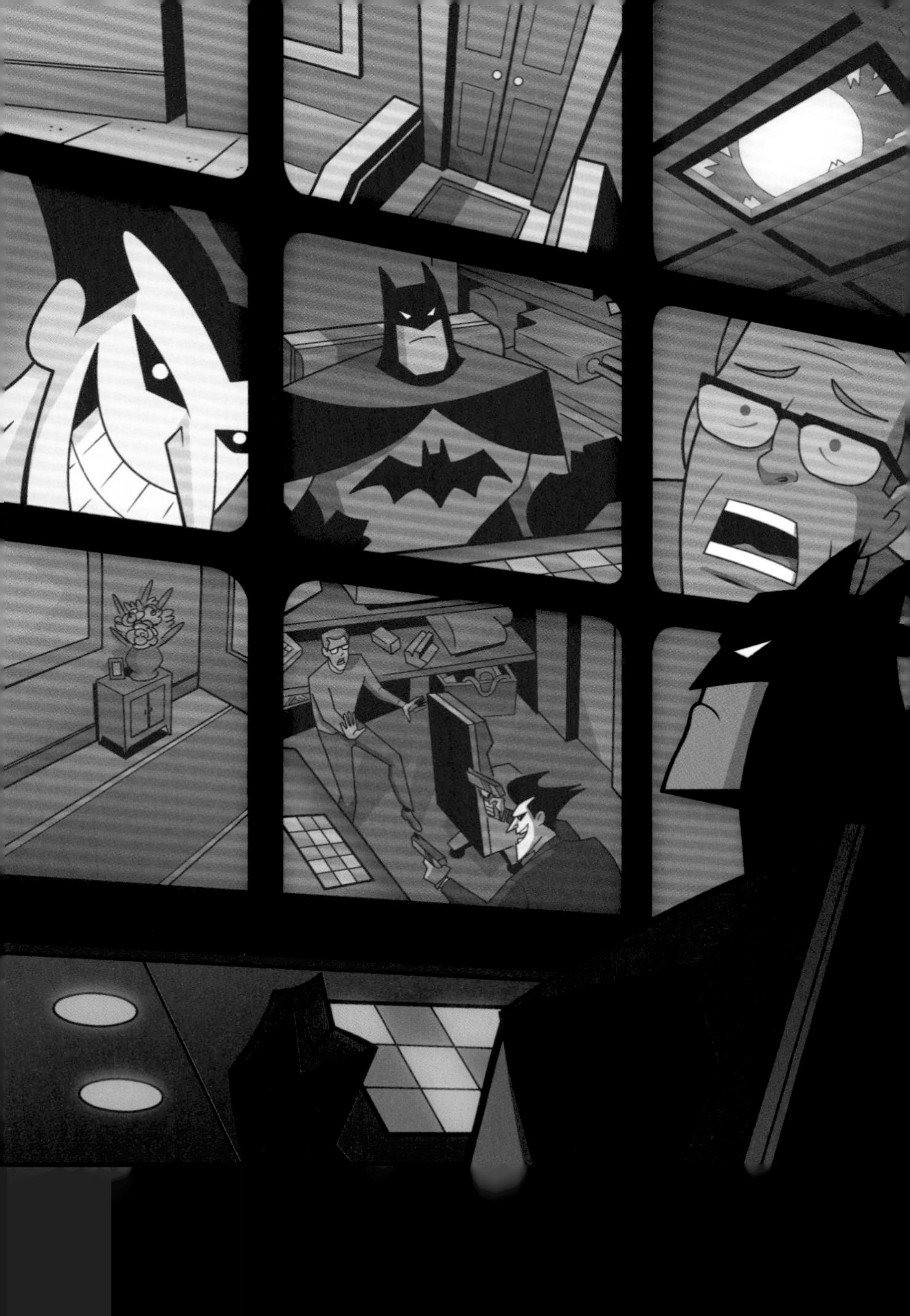

Batman shook his head. He'd hit a dead end.

"I think I need to visit an old friend," Batman said to himself.

CHAPTER 4

ARKHAM ASYLUM

CRRRRRRRRRRREAK!

The locked gates of Arkham Asylum opened as the Batmobile approached. The asylum's staff had never been able to figure out how Batman got the security gates to open for him. Little did they know that no one could keep the Dark Knight out.

Batman got out of the Batmobile. He looked up at the enormous, gothic building. It was home to some of the most dangerous criminals in the world.

Poison Ivy, Mr. Freeze, Bane, Killer Croc, Two-Face . . . the list went on and on and on.

It was also where the Joker was supposed to be right now. But every time he was caught, he managed somehow to escape the asylum. There was another prisoner inside who was nearly as deranged and dangerous as the Joker. And Batman thought he just might be able to help.

Batman made his way through the darkened hallways in silence. Soon, he reached a particular holding cell.

"Riddler," Batman said softly.

Edward Nigma, better known as the Riddler, looked up in surprise. "Well, isn't this unexpected," he said.

"Then again, when have you ever done the expected? I guess the unexpected is to be expected when it comes to the big bad Batman."

Batman paused. In a whispery, gravelly voice, he said, "I need your help."

The Riddler blinked once, then twice. "You . . . you need what?" he asked.

"You heard me," Batman said through gritted teeth.

"I did," the Riddler said, nodding his head. "But I'm finding it a bit hard to believe." The villain got up and began to pace his small cell. "I would suspect this is a trap if I weren't already imprisoned."

He ran a hand over his head. "Riddle me this, Batman: Why should I, the master of puzzles, help you? You put me here."

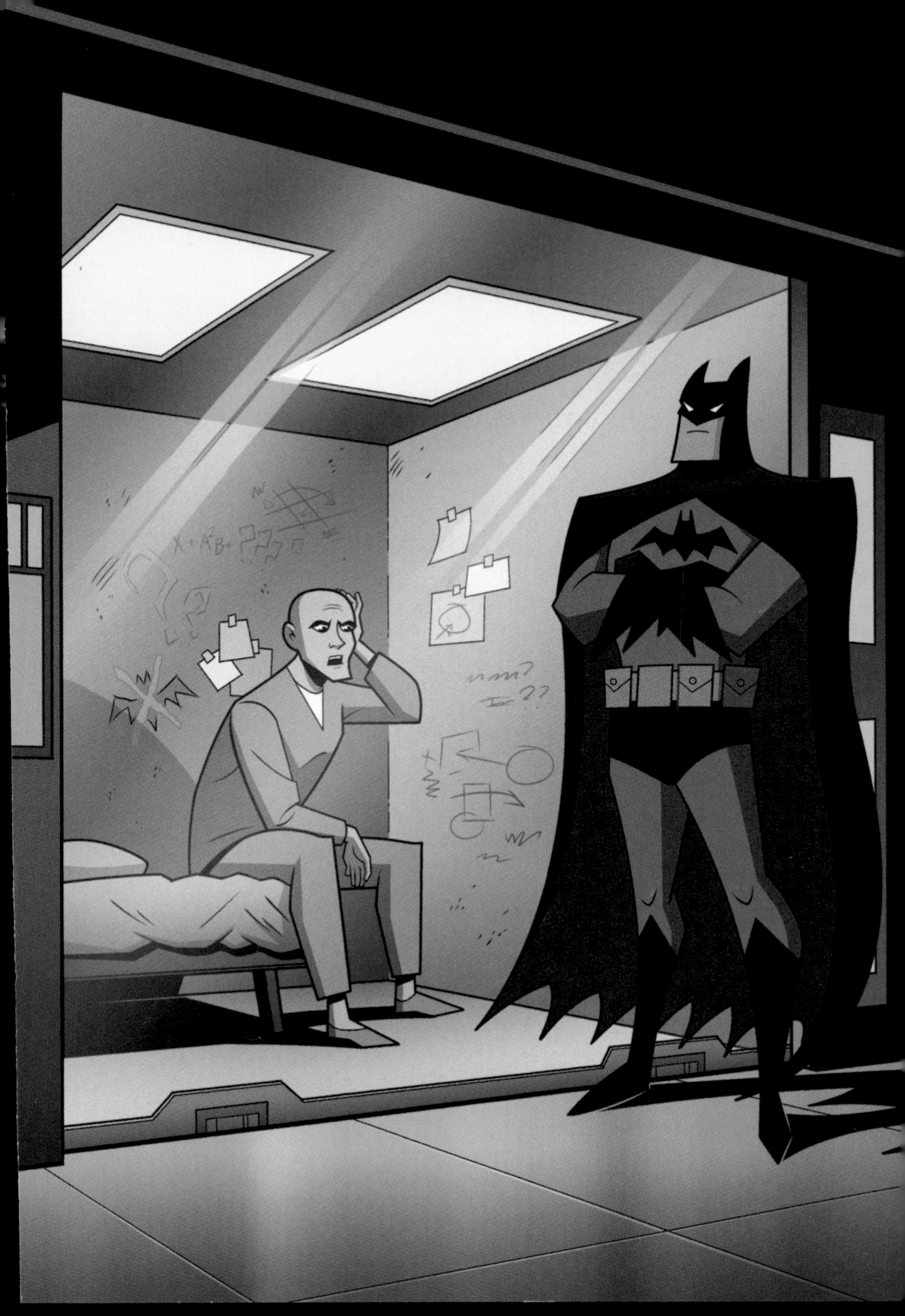

Batman tilted his head. "Let me explain the problem first," he said. "And then you can decide for yourself if you want to help or not."

The Riddler frowned. "No deal, Bats," he said. "You can't give me anything I want."

"I understand," the Batman said. He turned to leave.

"No, wait!" the Riddler cried, rushing forward, trying to catch the Batman before he pulled one of his trademark disappearing acts.

"What?" Batman said roughly as he turned to face Riddler's cell again.

Without meaning to, the Riddler jumped back. Even safe in a cell, Batman made him nervous.

The Riddler spat. "Mean of you to play with my curiosity like that," he said. "Let's hear it."

"It's the Joker," Batman said.

"Well, of course it is," the Riddler said impatiently. "He's not here, which means he's up to something. And if there's a problem you can't solve, the odds say that it's most likely that pasty freak."

"He's found a way to deliver his Joker Venom through a video game," Batman said.

"What, like they release a gas cloud?" Riddler asked.

"No," the Batman said. "At a certain point in the game, the player suddenly freezes and begins to grin like they've been doused with Joker Venom."

"Ah," the Riddler said, nodding. "So it's actually in the game code somehow. Well. That's smart. That's very smart."

He wiggled his fingers as though he was playing a game. Batman waited a moment, and then he said, "Well?"

"Hush," the Riddler replied, not looking up. "I'm thinking. These things take time."

Riddler was silent for a moment. Then he raised his head and spoke. "It'd be easier to solve this little puzzle if I were out of this horrible place."

"Not a chance," Batman said.

"At least give me a game system," Riddler said.

"No," Batman said.

The Riddler shrugged. "Can't blame a guy for trying."

"Riddler," the Batman said slowly. "Can you help?"

"Oh, absolutely," the Riddler said. "The question now is: What's in it for me? I mean, you already said I'm not getting out of here, so why should I help you?"

"Because," Batman said, "it'll prove you're smarter than the Joker."

The Riddler stared at the Batman. Then he burst out laughing. "You are good, Batman," he said. "I don't enjoy admitting that. But you're good." The Riddler lay down on his bunk. "Here's the thing. My guess is that he's figured out a way to implant something in there, triggering a reaction in the brain."

The Riddler got up and started pacing again.

"You know how flashing lights can trigger a seizure in people?" Riddler asked. "I'm guessing he found a way to do something similar."

"So . . .?" Batman prodded.

Riddler sat down and leaned back against the wall of his cell. "So there really is no way to fix this without actually digging into the computer code. All you can do is try to get the word out to people to stop playing."

The Riddler laughed. "But people being people, my guess is that there will always be fools willing to take a chance, thinking they're immune. People are so arrogant."

Batman smiled. "Yes, they are," the hero said.

The Riddler looked up uneasily. There was no sign of the Dark Knight.

"I hate when he does that," the Riddler said.

*   *   *

An hour later, every video game forum on the Internet had the same message posted.

Joker,

Showdown. Ninja Nemesis. *Tonight at midnight. You and me.*

If you dare.

— Batman

NINJA NEMESIS MESSAGE B
Name:
Batman
Email:
Website:
Message:
Joker,
Showdown. Ninja Nemesis. Tonight at midnight.
You and me.
If you dare.
— Batman

CHAPTER 5

GAME OVER

Alfred sighed. "Explain this to me again, if you'd be so kind," he said.

"There two ways to play the game," Batman said. "You can play against the computer, or you can play against another player in real time."

"I see. And having been issued a public challenge by the legendary Batman, the Joker will have no choice but to respond," Alfred said.

Batman nodded. "Exactly."

"And will you actually be playing the game?" Alfred asked.

"In a way," Batman said. "In any case, he'll be playing right into my hands."

Alfred blinked in surprise. "You know how to play *Ninja Nemesis*?"

Batman shook his head. "No clue," he said.

"Well," Alfred said, shaking his head. "That should make things rather interesting."

"Don't worry, Alfred," Batman said. "I have a plan."

*   *   *

As midnight approached, Internet servers worldwide were filled with activity.

Few people could even send or receive email, much less log on to watch the eagerly anticipated battle. Everyone was waiting for the big showdown to start.

With a few more keystrokes, Batman had put the game up on the main screen in Gotham Square. Even at midnight, it was Gotham City's busiest intersection. And tonight it was filled to the brim with excited observers.

The clock struck twelve. "Well," Alfred said. "It's time, sir."

Batman nodded. "Let's do it," he said.

A moment later, the crowd in Gotham Square began to cheer as Batman's avatar appeared on the huge screen. Immediately, the Joker's avatar joined him.

The crowd in Gotham Square grew quiet as the game started. The first level was by far the easiest — the players had to race across a giant stone bridge without falling off the edge. Additionally, the bridge was collapsing behind them, and each player could punch and kick the other player, slowing them down temporarily. The first one to the other side won the level.

The Joker made it across in a matter of seconds. Batman's avatar fell off the edge of the bridge after a well-timed Joker kick.

PLAYER TWO WINS! Appeared across the screen in big, bold red letters. Joker's avatar did a little celebratory dance.

A moment later, someone in the crowd said, "Fail."

"What's he doing?" someone else asked.

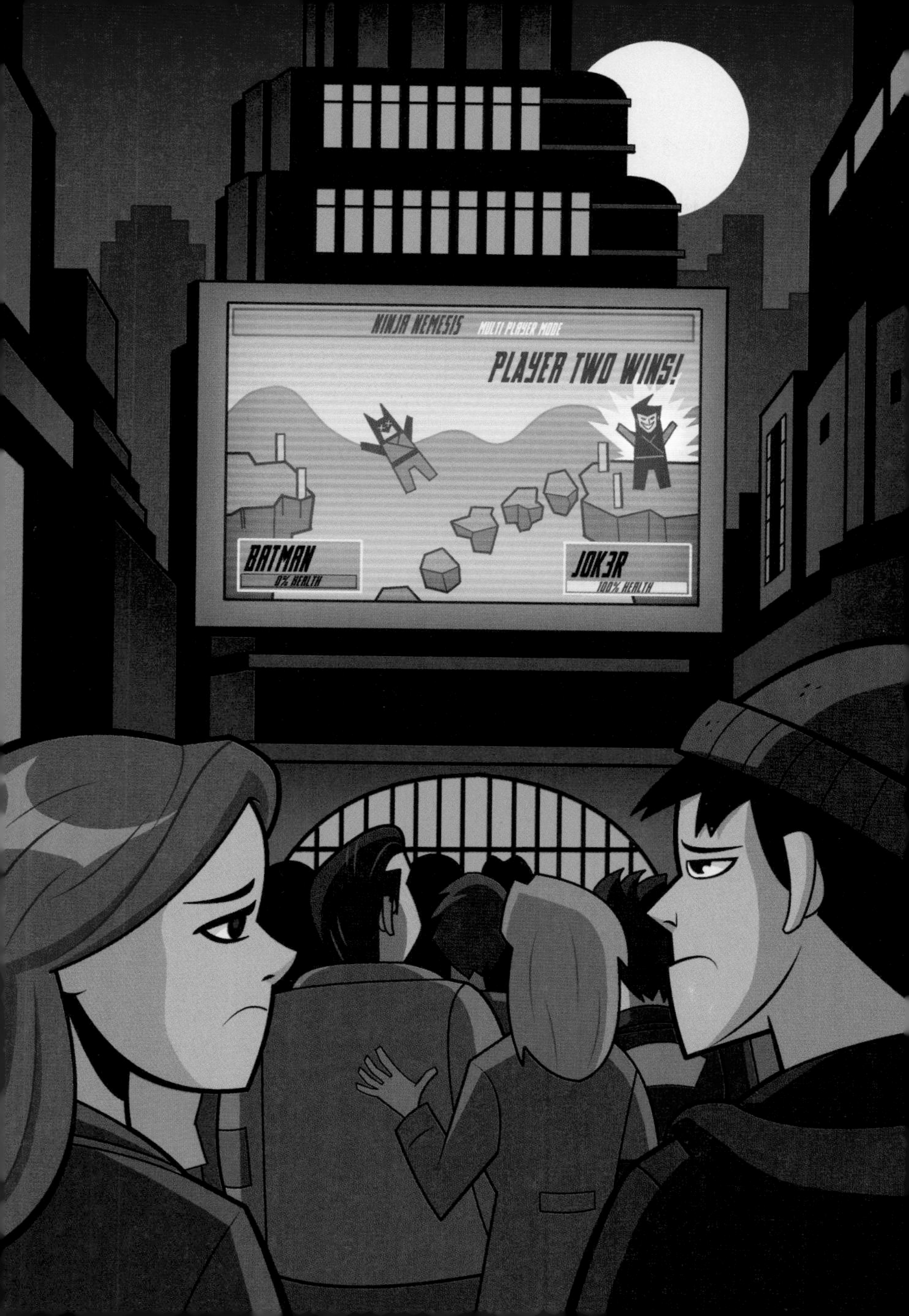
NINJA NEMESIS
MULTI PLAYER MODE
PLAYER TWO WINS!
BATMAN
0% HEALTH
JOK3R
100% HEALTH

A teen girl shook her head. "Losing," she said. "That can't really be Batman."

"Why not?" her friend asked, never taking his eyes off the screen.

"Because he's Batman," she said, as though it were obvious. "Batman can do anything."

"Except play video games," her friend laughed. "Man, he's awful!"

It was true. Batman was losing the game. The Joker was destroying him, winning every level easily. The warehouse level, the helicopter level, even the hospital rescue level. It wasn't even close.

In his hideout in the area of Gotham known as Little Odessa, the Joker giggled. "It feels pretty good to beat Bats for once!" he said. "Don't you agree, Mr. Young?"

Jonathan Young, the game's designer, watched unhappily. He grunted in disapproval.

"Oh, come on," the Joker said. "Sure, I know it's not pleasant being my captive and all tied up. But look on the bright side — you get a front row seat to watch me exhibit my elite skills!"

"Pfft," Jonathan said.

The Joker's grin faded. "I'd highly recommend admiring my elite skills," he warned.

Jonathan tried to clap his hands, but the ropes he was tied up with were too tight. He struggled in vain to slap them together.

"I have to tell you," the Joker said. "It doesn't seem like you really mean it."

Jonathan sighed.

"What's fun about beating someone who's obviously never played the game before?" Jonathan asked.

The Joker looked at Jonathan like he was crazy. "The point is to win," Joker said. "Who cares how or why?"

Jonathan shrugged.

SLAMMMMM! The Joker pushed his keyboard away. "Well, now you're just taking all the joy out of it," he said.

Jonathan rolled his eyes. "You're still playing," he said.

"So?" the Joker asked.

"So if you're not careful, he could still win," Jonathan said.

"Oh, please," the Joker said. "I've got this in the bag. I don't even need to look. Watch this."

The Joker very dramatically covered his eyes. As soon as he did, he thought he heard a shuffling noise.

The Joker took his hands off his eyes. Jonathan Young was gone.

"Well," the Joker said. "Now I am impressed. I had no idea you could disappear like that."

The Joker tapped his lips. "You can't disappear like that. Which means . . ." He grinned and jumped to his feet, ready for a fight. "You are a tricky one, aren't you . . . Batman?!"

But there was no sign of the Dark Knight.

The Joker tapped his foot. "Hey," he called. "Batman. I'm waiting. This is the part where we fight."

"Come on" the Joker cried. "I haven't got all night!"

"Sorry," the Dark Knight said from behind him. "Had a few things to take care of first."

The Joker suddenly kicked out at Batman. The Dark Knight dodged the kick, but by then the Joker had grabbed the computer from the desk. He threw it at Batman.

WOOOOOOOSH!

Batman dodged the computer easily. **CRUNCCCCCCCH!** It hit the wall and shattered.

"Well," said Batman with a smirk. "There goes the video game. Does that mean you give up?"

The Joker's eyes bulged with rage.

"Never!" the Joker screamed.

The Joker leaned forward. Acid squirted from the flower on his jacket lapel. The acid coasted harmlessly over the Batman's head and hit the wall.

HISSSSSSSSSSSSSSSS!

Batman narrowed his eyes. Faster than the Joker could regain his balance, the Dark Knight surged forward with a straight punch.

POW! The Joker was hit square in the jaw. He flew backward and landed on his back but quickly scrambled back to his feet.

"Is that the best you've got, Batman?" the Joker taunted. He lifted his fists, revealing he held a jagged piece of broken glass from the broken computer monitor.

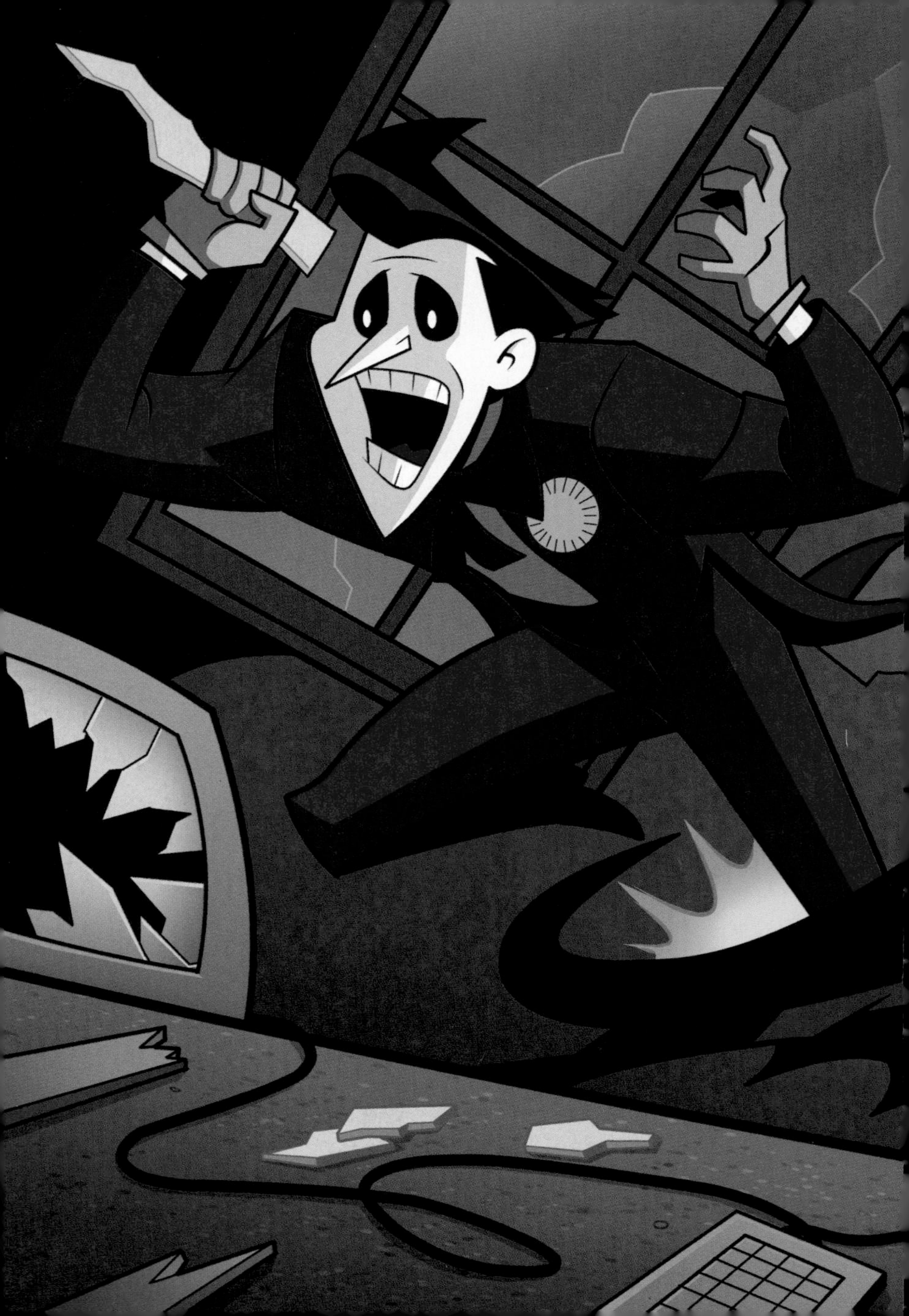

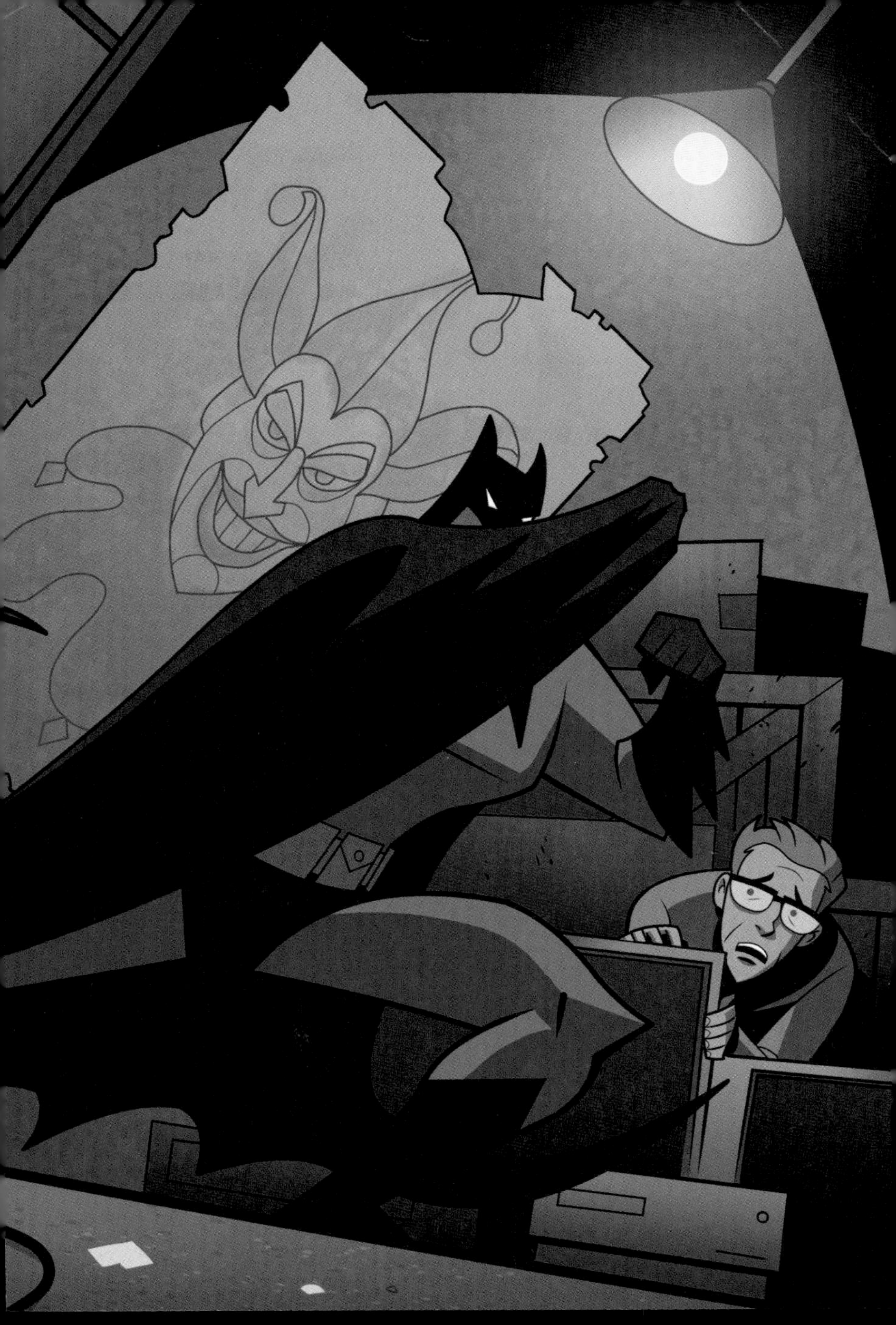

ROAAAAAAAAAAAAAAR!

The Joker let out a scream as he charged at Batman, slicing left and right with his makeshift weapon.

At the last second, Batman sidestepped. **FWIPPPP!** Batman knocked the Joker off his feet with a leg sweep. The clown went down with a resounding **THUDDDDD!** The piece of glass skittered across the floor and out of reach.

Batman stood over the Joker and looked down at him. He was groaning and holding his head.

After a moment, with great effort, the Joker opened his eyes. He glared up at Batman, teeth clenched tight.

Batman leaned down. "Game over," he said with a grin.

*   *   *

Tim Drake opened his eyes. He looked up at the strange ceiling, then around the room.

Bruce Wayne got up from the chair near the door and came over to Tim's bed. "Welcome back," he said.

"How long have I been out?" Tim whispered.

Bruce handed him a glass of water. "A few days," he answered. "Glad to have you back in the land of the living."

Tim took a sip. "What happened to me?" he asked.

"The Joker embedded a digital version of his Joker Venom in your video game," Bruce said.

Tim narrowed his eyes. He was struggling to tell if Bruce was making one of his very rare jokes. "Seriously?" he asked, baffled.

Bruce nodded. "He kidnapped the game's creator and forced him to embed corrupted code in the game. At random points, the Joker's game code triggered responses in the brain that were just like the Joker Venom. The only way to beat the Joker was to play him in a public, one-on-one game of *Ninja Nemesis*."

"So who beat him?" Tim asked.

"Batman did," said Alfred, smirking, as he entered the room.

"No way!" Tim said.

"Yes way," replied Alfred. "One could say he beat the Joker at his own game."

Bruce chuckled. "And I thought my jokes were bad, Alfred," he said.

"I can't believe I missed that!" said Tim. "I would have loved to have been there to see it."

Tim put his hands behind his head. Then he sat up. "Wait, Batman played a video game?" he said in disbelief.

Bruce and Alfred looked at each other. "Well, not exactly," Bruce said.

"But you said —" Tim began.

"I never said that Batman actually played him," corrected Alfred.

Tim shook his head in confusion. "I don't understand," he said. "Then who did play the Joker?"

Bruce smirked.

"While Batman appeared to be fighting a very public duel with the Joker," Bruce said, "I was actually tracing the Joker's IP address. See, the only way to take the video game down was by finding the Joker."

Alfred smiled. "A brilliant plan, really," he said. "The Joker thought he was competing in a video game with the Dark Knight, but really Batman was using the opportunity to track him down."

"Ah," Tim said. "So the game was just a trick. Very nice."

Bruce said, "Once I rescued the game's designer, Jonathan Young, I —"

"Whoa!" Tim interrupted. "You actually met Jonathan Young?"

Bruce nodded. "I did," he said.

"Man," Tim said. "Some guys have all the luck."

"Yes," Alfred said. "Kind of like being lucky enough to be Robin the Boy Wonder."

Tim laughed.

Bruce cleared his throat. "As I was saying, Jonathan was able to pull all the online copies of the game off the web. He also released a game update that overrode the Joker code."

Tim stretched, and then froze again. "So, if you were actually tracking the Joker, then who was really playing?"

Bruce held his hand out toward Alfred and smiled.

"What?" Tim said. "Alfred? You played *Ninja Nemesis* with the Joker? I don't believe it!"

"And why not?" Alfred asked.

Tim said. "It's just kind of ironic," he said. "You're the one who's always saying that video games will rot my mind."

Alfred let out a laugh, but quickly straightened his cuffs and composed himself. "And once again, I am proven correct," he said. "I'd say this game definitely did rot your mind. At least for a little while."

Tim laughed. "I guess you're right," he said. "So everything's back to normal now?"

Bruce nodded. "The Joker's back in Arkham Asylum, the game is fixed, and Jonathan Young has a new job."

"Oh," Tim said. "What is it?"

"He works for Wayne Enterprises now," Bruce said. "Heading up our brand new video game division. His first project is something called *Alien Clown Attack*. It's a kid's game. The objective is to stop extra-terrestrial clowns from invading Earth."

Tim burst out laughing. "The Joker's going to hate that so much!" he said.

Bruce smiled. "I know."

THE JOKER

REAL NAME:
Unknown

OCCUPATION:
Professional Criminal

BASE:
Gotham City

HEIGHT:
6 feet 5 inches

WEIGHT:
192 pounds

EYES:
Green

HAIR:
Green

The Clown Prince of Crime. The Ace of Knaves. Batman's most dangerous enemy is known by many names, but he answers to no one. After falling into a vat of toxic waste, this once lowly criminal was transformed into an evil madman. The chemical bath bleached his skin, dyed his hair green, and peeled back his lips into a permanent grin. Since then, the Joker has only one purpose in life . . . to destroy Batman. In the meantime, however, he's happy tormenting the good people of Gotham City.

- The Joker always wants the last laugh. To get it, he's devised dozens of deadly clown tricks. He has even gone as far as faking his own death!

- Always the trickster, the Joker designs all of his weapons to look comical in order to conceal their true danger. This trickery usually gets a chuckle or two from his foes, giving the Joker an opportunity to strike first.

- The Clown Prince of Crime has spent more time in Arkham Asylum than any Gotham criminal. But that doesn't mean he's comfortable behind bars. He has also escaped more times than anyone.

- While at Arkham, the Joker met Dr. Harleen Quinzel. She fell madly in love and aided the crazy clown in his many escapes. Soon, she turned to a life of crime herself, as the evil jester Harley Quinn.

BIOGRAPHIES

SCOTT PETERSON got his start in comics at DC
Comics, editing their flagship title, *Detective Comics*
and launching the first of the Adventures sub-genre
of comics, *The Batman Adventures*. As a writer, he has
been published by Disney, Scholastic, Golden Books,
HarperCollins, and DC Comics, writing such books as
Batgirl, *Scooby-Doo*, and *The Gotham Adventures*.

MIKE CAVALLARO is originally from New Jersey, where
he attended the Joe Kubert School of Cartoon and
Graphic Art, and has worked in comics and animation
since the early 1990's. Mike's comics include "Parade
(with fireworks)", a Will Eisner Comics Industry Award-
nominee, "The Life and Times of Savior 28", written by
J.M. DeMatteis, and "Foiled", written by Jane Yolen. Mike
is a member of the National Cartoonists Society and
lives in Brooklyn, NY.

GLOSSARY

appreciate (uh-PREE-she-ate)—to enjoy or value somebody or something

avatar (AV-uh-tahr)—an electronic image that represents a computer user

captivating (KAP-ti-vay-ting)—if something is captivating, then it is delightful or holds your attention

grim (GRIM)—gloomy, stern, and unpleasant

intending (in-TEN-ding)—aiming to do something

ironic (eye-RON-ik)—if a situation is ironic, the actual result differs from the expected result

maniac (MAY-nee-ak)—someone who is insane or acts in a wild or violent manner

mayhem (MAY-hem)—a situation of confusion or violent destruction

skittered (SKIT-urd)—skimmed or bounced along a surface

triggered (TRIG-urd)—caused something to happen as a reaction

tuxedo (tuhk-SEE-doh)—a man's jacket worn with a bow tie for formal occasions

DISCUSSION QUESTIONS

1. Batman gets a lot of help in this book. Talk about the people who help him.

2. The Joker has a secret hideout. What kinds of things would you put in your secret hideout? Talk about your hideout.

3. This book has ten illustrations. Which one is your favorite? Why?

WRITING PROMPTS

1. Batman is a master of martial arts, detective work, and stealth or sneakiness. Of these three talents, which would you want to have the most? Write about what you'd do with your new talent.

2. Batman asks his enemy, the Riddler, for help. Have you ever had to work with someone you didn't like? Write about some cooperative experiences you've had.

3. Batman faces off against the Joker in the video game *Ninja Nemesis*. Design your own video game. What's it called? What happens in the game? Write about it.

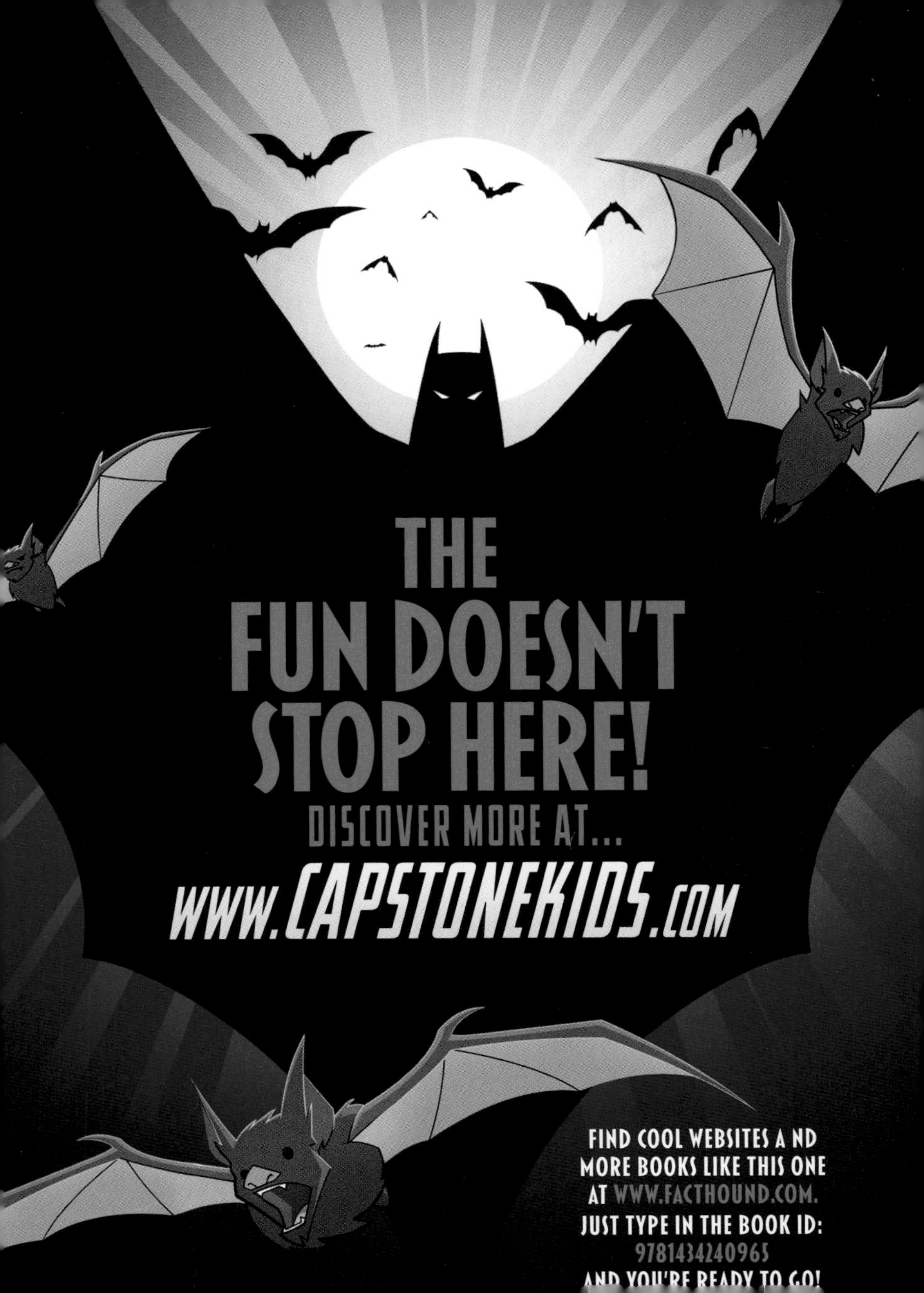
THE
FUN DOESN'T
STOP HERE!
DISCOVER MORE AT...
WWW.CAPSTONEKIDS.COM
FIND COOL WEBSITES A ND
MORE BOOKS LIKE THIS ONE
AT WWW.FACTHOUND.COM.
JUST TYPE IN THE BOOK ID:
9781434240965
AND YOU'RE READY TO GO!

LOOK FOR MORE

THE DARK KNIGHT™

CAT COMMANDER
BAILLIE • VECCHIO

SCARECROW'S
FLOCK OF FEAR
MANNING • VECCHIO

THE JOKER VIRUS

KILLER CROC OF DOOM!
SUTTON • VECCHIO